The Editorial Staff of
The Rodent's Gazette

1. Linda Thinslice
2. Sweetie Cheesetriangle
3. Ratella Redfur
4. Soya Mousehao
5. Cheesita de la Pampa
6. Coco Chocamouse
7. Mouseanna Mousetti
8. Patty Plumprat
9. Tina Spicytail
10. William Shortpaws
11. Valerie Vole
12. Trap Stilton
13. Dolly Fastpaws
14. Zeppola Zap
15. Merenguita Gingermouse
16. Shorty Tao
17. Baby Tao
18. Gigi Gogo
19. Teddy von Muffler
20. Thea Stilton
21. Erronea Misprint
22. Pinky Pick
23. Ya-ya O'Cheddar
24. Ratsy O'Shea
25. Geronimo Stilton
26. Benjamin Stilton
27. Briette Finerat
28. Raclette Finerat
29. Mousella MacMouser
30. Kreamy O'Cheddar
31. Blasco Tabasco
32. Toffie Sugarsweet
33. Tylerat Truemouse
34. Larry Keys
35. Michael Mouse

Geronimo Stilton
A learned and brainy
mouse; editor of
The Rodent's Gazette

Thea Stilton
Geronimo's sister and
special correspondent at
The Rodent's Gazette

Trap Stilton
An awful joker;
Geronimo's cousin and
owner of the store
Cheap Junk for Less

Benjamin Stilton
A sweet and loving
nine-year-old mouse;
Geronimo's favorite
nephew

Geronimo Stilton

SHIPWRECK ON THE PIRATE ISLANDS

Scholastic Inc.

New York   Toronto   London   Auckland   Sydney
Mexico City   New Delhi   Hong Kong   Buenos Aires

ISBN 0-439-69141-9

Text by Geronimo Stilton
Original title: *L'isola del tesoro fantasma*
Cover by Larry Keys
Illustrations by Johnny Stracchino and Mary Fontina
Graphics by Merenguita Gingermouse and Zeppola Zap
Special thanks to Kathryn Cristaldi
Interior design by Kay Petronio

12 11 10 9 8 7 6 5 4 3 2 1   5 6 7 8 9 10/0

Printed in the U.S.A.   08
First printing, April 2005

BUT WON'T IT BE ... DANGEROUS?

I was working peacefully in my office one morning when my sister burst through the door. Thea is the special correspondent at *The Rodent's Gazette*. What is the *Gazette*? Oops. *Sorry*, mouse fans. I forgot to introduce myself. My name is Stilton, *Geronimo Stilton*. I run a newspaper called *The Rodent's Gazette*. It is the most popular daily on Mouse Island.

"Drop everything, Geronimo!" Thea demanded. "We're going on a mini vacation!"

"Drop everything, Geronimo —
we're going on a mini vacation!"

I shook my head. I was way too *BUSY*. I had to meet with the printer. I had to meet with the photographer. I had to meet with the cafeteria mouse. I had found a tuft of fur in my macaroni and cheese last week. Yuck!

Just then, my favorite nephew, Benjamin, appeared. "Uncle, have you heard the news?" he squeaked happily. "We're all going on vacation! I'm so excited! This is going to be the best vacation of my whole life!"

How could I say no to my dear, sweet nephew? "Well, all right," I agreed. "Why don't we go to the *Soft Squeak Resort*? It's on a beautiful, relaxing island. . . ."

Before I could continue, my sister interrupted me. "Forget *Soft Squeak*, Gerry Berry. That place is for senior citizens," she scoffed. "We're going to the Pirate Islands. White beaches, crystal-clear water, and

jungles filled with wild animals! There are tigers, pythons, and even gigantic tarantulas!"

I shivered. "Um, well, the white beaches and crystal-clear water sound great. But won't all those wild animals **BE DANGEROUS?**"

Thea snickered. "Oh, Geronimoid, stop being such a SCAREDY MOUSE!" she scolded. "Go pack your suitcase. We'll meet at the airport in twenty minutes!"

Twenty minutes? I barely had time to comb my fur!

Ferocious tigers

Gigantic tarantulas

Terrifying pythons

THE PIRATE ISLANDS GUIDEBOOK

Luckily, I remembered to pack a guidebook on the **PIRATE ISLANDS**. I like to read about the places I visit.

I read about the PIRATES, too. This is what I learned.

Welcome to the Pirate Islands!

PIRATES

The Pirate Code

Many believe that pirates broke every law known to mice. But that is not exactly true. Pirates did obey some laws, but only ones that were established aboard their own ship. For example:

1. *The loot is to be divided equally among all pirates.*
2. *No pirate is allowed to gamble.*
3. *Every pirate must always be ready for battle.*
4. *No women and children are allowed on board.*
5. *Whoever steals or flees from combat will be punished by death.*

Privateers, Buccaneers, and Filibusters

After Christopher Columouse landed in America, there was an outbreak of piracy along the Caribbean coast and in the Antilles. There were several types of pirates.

Privateers were sailors who carried a letter, given by their king, authorizing them to attack enemy ships. In exchange for this document, they gave half of their booty to their sovereign.

Buccaneers were European pirates who attacked Spanish ships and settlements in the West Indies.

Filibusters were pirates of English, French, and Dutch origin who operated in the Caribbean.

Help, Pirate Overboard!

It seems incredible, but often pirates did not know how to swim. They prided themselves on dominating the seas without ever taking a bath.

For example, the pirate Bartholomew Portugues did not know how to swim, so he fled from a prison ship by floating to shore on a raft made of kegs.

The Jolly Roger

Whenever someone saw a pirate flag approaching, he would be so frightened that more often than not he would surrender without a fight!

Every commander had his own personal flag. These are the most famouse:

John Rackham (died 1720) "Calico Jack"

This English pirate liked to dress in calico. He would attack local merchants and fishing vessels in the Caribbean. Despite the pirate rule about no women on board, Calico Jack had not one but two women pirates disguised as men among his crew.

Calico Jack's flag

Bartholomew Roberts (1682-1722) "Black Bart"

This English pirate was probably the most successful pirate in history. He captured four hundred vessels and operated off the coast of South America and in the West Indies. He never drank or gambled and always went to bed early.

Black Bart's flag

Henry Avery (1665-1728) "Long Ben"

This Englishman was a pirate for only one year, but in that time he captured riches and booty from English, Indian, and Danish ships off the coasts of Africa and India. He is probably the only well-known pirate who was not killed in battle or ever caught for his crimes. But he died penniless after losing all his booty on land.

Long Ben's flag

Edward Teach (died 1718) "Blackbeard"

This Englishman turned pirate in 1713 and preyed on ships off the coast of the Carolinas and Virginia. He captured a large French merchantman, equipped her with forty guns, and renamed her *Queen Anne's Revenge*.

Blackbeard's flag

PIRATE ABCs

Aft: Toward the rear or stern of a boat.

Aweigh: The position of the anchor as it is raised clear of the bottom of the sea.

Batten down: Secure hatches and loose objects both within the hull and on deck.

Below: Beneath the deck.

Booty: Riches or valuables taken by force.

Bow: The forward part of a boat.

Bridge: The part of the ship from which the vessel is steered and its speed controlled.

Chart: A map used by navigators.

Course: The direction in which a boat is steered.

Deck: The permanent covering over a compartment, hull, or any part of the ship.

Doubloon: A gold coin once used in Spain and Spanish America.

Forward: Toward the bow of a boat.

Galley: The kitchen area of a boat.

Halyards: Lines used to hoist or lower sails or flags.

Jolly Roger: A pirate flag, usually with a skull-and-crossbones design.

Knot: A measure of speed equal to one nautical mile (6,076 feet) per hour.

Logbook: The ship's diary, used to record weather conditions, course, speed, and any relevant information about navigation and crew.

Mast: **A vertical pole used to support sails and their rigging.**

Port: **The left side of a boat when one is looking forward.**

Rudder: **A vertically hinged plate of metal or wood mounted at the stern of a vessel, which is used to steer its course.**

Sail: **A piece of cloth that catches or directs the wind and powers a vessel.**

Sea dog: **An experienced sailor.**

Shiver me timbers: **An expression of surprise or disbelief. When a ship strikes a rock hard, her timbers shiver.**

Shrouds: **Ropes used to support the masts.**

Starboard: **The right side of a boat when one is facing forward.**

Stern: **The rear end of a boat.**

Walk the plank: **To be forced to walk over the side of a ship into the sea.**

Mast · Top · Sails · Shrouds · Bridge · Halyards · Stern · Bow · Rudder · Hull · Cannons

Fin's Revenge

Littlecocoa

Motormeltdown

I continued to read the guidebook: "Some small islands are no longer inhabited. One such is **LITTLECOCOA**, on which only one coconut tree grows. On the island of *FIN'S REVENGE*, the waters near the beaches are infested with ferocious sharks.

"Around the isle of **Motormeltdown**, currents are so strong that the ships need to run the engine at full power so they don't crash against the cliffs. And then there's NO MOUSE'S LAND, an extremely small and uncharted island.

"Finally, the farthest and wildest of all of them is the island no airplane dares to fly to and where no ship ever docks, and

No Mouse's Land

where no one would dream of going . . . the island of Thump Flop, where numerous **Plop** birds live.

Here, according to legend, a pirate hid a treasure right on the —"

My reading was interrupted by someone squeaking my name. It was my cousin Trap.

"SHAKE A PAW, GERMEISTER!"

he shrieked. Everyone in the airport turned and stared.

One thing you should know about Trap. He is the loudest, most *obnoxious* mouse in the world! Even worse, he loves to pick on me.

I cringed. So much for a relaxing vacation.

I would be lucky if I made it home with all of my whiskers!

A MOST BIZARRE MOUSE

The plane landed thirteen hours later. My stomach was in knots, and not nautical knots, if you know what I mean! Did I mention I'm AFRAID of flying?

A small hydroplane was waiting to take us to a place called Loot Island. According to my guidebook, the island was small and totally uncivilized. That meant no lights. No running water. No cheese logs by the pool. I sighed. Oh, how I love a nice cheddar cheese log.

My thoughts were interrupted by a most bizarre-looking rodent. He had lots of **curly black hair** and was dressed in PURPLE shorts and a neon YELLOW

MAP OF THE PIRATE ISLANDS

A = PAWSOFFTHEGOLD
B = FIN'S REVENGE
C = ANCHOR ARCH
D = MOTORMELTDOWN
E = BUCCANEER'S COVE
F = NO MOUSE'S LAND
G = LITTLECOCOA
H = TREASURE TRAP

I = WINDY POINT
J = SAILOR'S DELIGHT
K = ANCHORS AWEIGH ISLE
L = LOOT ISLAND
M = CAPTAIN'S CURSE
N = PARROT ISLE
O = THUMP FLOP
X = BURIED TREASURE

shirt with **RED** hearts. Around his neck hung a huge gold medal with the word *SCRAM!* printed on it.

"Yo, Mousey Mouse!" he greeted me and stuck out one chubby paw. I noticed a *s h a r k* -tooth bracelet dangling from his wrist. "The name's ROUGH RAT RICKY, but everyone calls me BOUNCER," he announced.

He squeezed my paw so hard, my eyes nearly popped out of my fur. Rancid rat hairs! That mouse had some shake. He was crushing every bone in my paw! I wouldn't be able to write for weeks!

I was about to complain when I noticed

ROUGH RAT RICKY, aka BOUNCER.

his tattoos. On his left arm, there was a picture of a hideous dragon. On his right arm, there was a ferocious cat with blood dripping from its jaws.

I gulped. Yes, they were only *TATTOOS* — but they looked so real! What kind of a mouse liked such terrifying tattoos? I stared up at Bouncer. That's when I saw his ear. It looked like it had been chewed by a CAT! No, I wasn't going to mess with this rodent.

Just then, Bouncer smacked me hard on the back. My whiskers nearly flew off my snout.

"Ready to leave, Mousey Mouse?" he chuckled.

I tried to squeak, but no sound came out. Bouncer had knocked the wind out of me.

SCRAM! MOVE IT! GET LOST!

Bouncer bounded onto the hydroplane. He patted a photo on the dashboard with his stubby paw. It was a picture of an older female mouse with hair just like Bouncer's. "Hi, **MOMSY WOMSY!**" he cooed. He blew the picture a kiss. Then he stared at the controls. "Frozen cheddar cheese pops!" he shrieked suddenly. "I've forgotten how to turn on the engine!"

My jaw hit the ground. "Wh-wh-what d-d-did you s-s-s-say?" I stammered.

Bouncer winked at me. "Just pulling your paw,

I AM BOUNCER'S MOM.

Mousey Mouse!" he chuckled.

I grabbed my cousin's paw. "Couldn't you have found a normal pilot?" I asked softly. "This one is so strange. WON'T IT BE DANGEROUS FLYING WITH HIM?"

Trap just smirked. "All pilots are strange. Look at your sister," he remarked. "She's one of the strangest mice I know."

Thea jumped to her paws. My sister is a licensed pilot. She even has her own plane.

"HOW DARE YOU!" she squeaked at Trap. Before I knew it, the two of them were at each other's throats.

I sighed. Meanwhile, BOUNCER began preparing for takeoff. First he checked the controls. Then he checked his seat belt. Then he checked his hair with a pocket mirror. "Looking good!"

I stared anxiously out the window. The

sky was growing CLOUDY.
Very CLOUDY.

"The weather doesn't look so great.
WON'T IT BE DANGEROUS flying in all of
these clouds?" I asked Thea.

She just scoffed. "I'm sure Bouncer called
the control tower. They check on the weather.
If they say we can leave, then we leave.
Don't be such a SCAREDY MOUSE,
Germeister."

I couldn't help it. The sky was getting
darker and darker. It looked like we
were about to fly into a big storm. Was it a
thunderstorm? I hate thunderstorms. At
home, I hide under my bed when there is a
thunderstorm.

Suddenly, Bouncer stuck his head out of
the window. He waved a paw at everybody
on the runway. "**SCRAM! MOVE IT! GET LOST!**"

he shrieked. Then he turned on the plane, and we shot off into the sky.

As soon as we were airborne, he smacked his forehead with his paw. "Cheese niblets!" he squeaked. "I forgot to get gas!"

My stomach dropped. "No g-g-gas?" I stammered.

Bouncer roared with laughter. "Just pulling your paw, Mousey Mouse!"

I chewed my whiskers. Oh, why did I agree to come on this awful vacation? I could have been relaxing at the *Soft Squeak Resort*. I could have been playing shuffleboard. I could have been getting a massage. Instead I was listening to a crazy mouse telling warped jokes.

This wasn't a vacation. It was a **NIGHTMARE!**

I Told You So . . .

After an hour, the sky turned completely black. The plane began to shake violently. The wind roared. It screamed. It wound my tail up in knots. Oh, no, that wasn't the wind. That was me. I wind my tail when I'm nervous. I really should break the habit. Thea says it makes your fur fall out. I hope she's wrong. Have you ever seen a mouse with no fur? Let me tell you, it is not a pretty sight.

Bouncer's voice interrupted my thoughts. "Control tower, what's the deal with this weather?" he shouted.

The radio **CRACKLED**. "Tornado . . . headed . . . right . . . for . . . you!!!" a voice screamed. "EMERGENCY!"

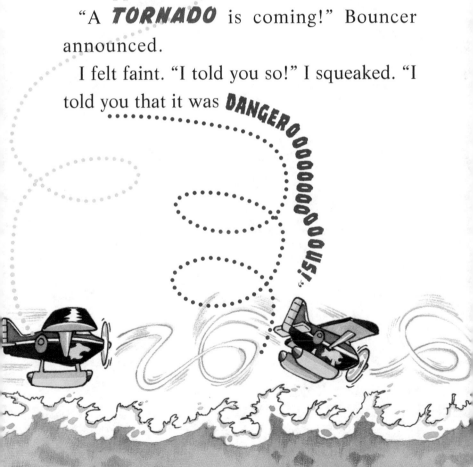

Everyone turned as PALE as a ball of mozzarella. Well, everyone except me. That's because I was already PALE. The blood had frozen under my fur the minute I'd stepped on board!

"A **TORNADO** is coming!" Bouncer announced.

I felt faint. "I told you so!" I squeaked. "I told you that it was DANGEROOOOOOOOOOOOOOUS!"

Nose Down into the Deep Blue Waves

I helped Benjamin put on a life jacket.

No one was talking. How unusual. Normally, you can't get the Stilton family to stop squeaking. Everyone stared worriedly at the sky. It grew **darker** and **darker**.

The wind blew furiously. The plane lurched and swayed. **SWISH...SWISHH...SWISHHH...**

I held on to Benjamin's tiny paw for dear life.

"Don't worry, little nephew," I whispered. "We'll be just fine." I hoped he couldn't hear my teeth chattering. Or see my fur standing on end. Or feel my paw trembling. Rat-munching rattlesnakes! I was scared silly!

Suddenly, Bouncer pointed the plane's nose toward land.

"Hang on!" he screamed. "I'm going to try to make an *EMERGENCY* landing!"

The wind grew stronger and stronger. The waves grew closer and closer.

Seconds later, a gust of wind sent the plane plunging into the deep blue waves.

GLUB . . . BLUB, BLUB, BLUB!

The plane crashed into the sea with a loud splash. Instantly, we began to sink. GLUB . . . BLUB, BLUB, BLUB!

We tried to open the door. It wouldn't budge.

Then I remembered something I had read in one of my favorite books. In the book, the hero accidentally drives off a bridge. His car sinks underwater. The water pressure is too strong for him to escape. He has to wait until the car goes completely under.

Before long, the water had covered our plane. I pushed with all of my strength. And the door opened! Isn't reading amazing?

I took a deep breath. Then I grabbed

We tried to open the door . . . but only when the plane was filled with water . . . then were we able to escape!

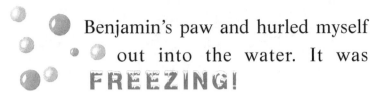

Benjamin's paw and hurled myself out into the water. It was **FREEZING!**

I started swimming. The **water** was darker than my mouse hole at midnight. I couldn't see my own fur in front of my face. But I could see bubbles. They were coming from my mouth. I followed them up to the surface.

"We made it!" I spluttered, giving Benjamin a hug.

Thea and Trap popped up next to me. But there was no sign of Bouncer.

I looked around and spotted a small island not too far away. We swam to shore. Then we collapsed onto the sand.

Water dripped down my whiskers. I was so tired, I couldn't move. That was a good thing, because I wanted to strangle my sister for bringing me on this *NIGHTMARE* vacation!

NOTHING CAN STOP THE STILTON FAMILY!

The SUN was about to rise. I was feeling hopeful.

Then I heard someone sobbing. It was Trap. "What if we're trapped here forever?" he MOANED. "I'll never go to another mouseball game again. I'll never see my friends. I'll never eat another cheddar melt at the All U Can Eat Cheese Palace."

Did I mention my cousin loves to eat? And eat . . . and eat . . .

Thea rolled her eyes. "Get a grip, Trap," she squeaked. "We Stiltons never give up."

Benjamin smiled. "Aunt Thea's right, Cousin Trap," he nodded. "Nothing can stop the Stilton family!"

With a sigh, Trap got a grip on himself. Then we twisted our tails together and shouted,

"Nothing can stop the Stilton family!"

We came up with a list of chores. Trap was in charge of getting the food. Thea gathered WOOD to light the fire. Benjamin made little skirts out of palm leaves so we'd have something to wear (our clothes were soaking wet). And I built a shelter under a coconut tree.

coconut tree

It was a hard day. The sun ROASTED my fur. The wind tangled my whiskers. My paws sprouted a thousand blisters. Well, OK, maybe not a thousand blisters. But you get the picture. It was hard work.

I stared at the ocean. It looked so cool and inviting. But I was afraid. What if a shark

Plop! Plop! Plop!

attacked me? What if a jellyfish stung me? What if my grass skirt floated away?

Just then, something **plopped** onto my head.

Seconds later, there were more **plops**.

PLOP! PLOP! PLOP!

The sky had filled with a swarm of birds. They looked just like seagulls.

"Squawk,
   squawk,
      squawk!" the birds called.

Benjamin quickly handed out little umbrellas made of leaves. He was getting pretty good with those leaves. First the skirts. Then the umbrellas. What next? Shirts? Neckties? Maybe someday Benjamin would grow up to be a designer. "Never leaf home without your Benjamin Stilton." Hmm . . . maybe he was onto something.

I Am Rodent, Hear Me Squeak!

Just then, another **plop** hit my umbrella. It reminded me of the guidebook on the **PIRATE ISLANDS**. It talked about the plop birds on an island called Thump Flop.

"I know where we are!" I cried excitedly. "We're on Thump Flop Island. I read about it in the guidebook. It said the island had plants and edible fruits."

Thea grinned. "Good work, Gerry Berry," she squeaked. "I guess it pays to have a bookmouse for a brother sometimes."

I was about to remind her that my name is not Gerry Berry when I remembered something else. I had read a few more interesting things in that guidebook.

"In ancient times, pirates brought their gold and riches to the Pirate Islands. Many treasures are still buried there. There are also many ghosts on the islands. The ghost of the famous pirate Silverpaw wanders the beaches on the island of Thump Flop. His ship was said to have mysterious powers. It could appear and disappear in the blink of an eye."

That night, I curled up in a big palm leaf to sleep. It wasn't easy. I kept thinking about pirates and ghosts and disappearing ships. *Don't be such a scaredy mouse,* I scolded myself. I sang a little song to give myself courage: **"I AM BRAVE. I AM STRONG. I AM RODENT, HEAR ME SQUEAK."**

My cousin Trap mimicked me in a singsong voice. **"I AM BRAVE. I AM STRONG. I AM RODENT, HEAR ME SNORE!"**

You Have a Leech on Your Face!

The next day, we decided to explore the island. We headed down a long, *sandy* path. It led into a **THICK MANGROVE FOREST**. My paws sank into the damp sand. It was hard to walk.

Suddenly, I noticed something odd. Huge holes were opening up in the sand. The holes were filled with gigantic crabs. Their pincerlike claws swiped at us as we scampered by.

mangrove forest

"𝕳oley cheese!" I cried out. My heart began to race. Sweat rolled down my fur. Do you like crabs? I don't. They always look angry. I hate those razor-sharp claws. And their beady little eyes look so **SINISTER**.

No one else seemed to be bothered by the crabs. Trap was even humming a silly tune.

Just then, something slimy and wet hit me in the face.

"A **LEECH!** Geronimo, you have an enormouse leech on your face!" hollered Trap.

I began to see stars. "**Heeeeeelp!**" I shrieked. I ripped the wet leech off my face. Then I stared at it in my paw.

"B-b-but this isn't a leech," I blabbered. "It's a wet handkerchief."

Trap was jumping up and down all around me, roaring with *laughter*.

I should have known. Have I told you my cousin loves to play tricks on me?

"Ha-ha-ha! You fell for it, Germeister!" he spluttered. "You're so easy to fool. It's like taking Cheesy Chews from a mouseling!"

I ran after him. "If I catch you, you'll never eat another Cheesy Chew again!" I shouted.

Oh, how did I get stuck with such an obnoxious mouse for a relative?

BIGGER THAN FIFTY SUMO RAT WRESTLERS!

Trap was still laughing as he ran down the path. Then he turned to **make a face** at me. That's when his face went PALE.

"Ge-Ge-Geromino . . . d-d-don't move . . ." he stuttered. "There's a gigantic c-c-crab behind you!"

I snorted. You can fool this mouse sometimes, but I'm no cheesebrain. I mean, I wasn't born yesterday. I know when someone is pulling my paw. "Enough kidding around, Trap," I said, laughing. "I know there's no *giant crab*."

My cousin's eyes were nearly popping out of their sockets. I had to give it to him. He really did look scared. I wondered if he had

been taking acting lessons in his spare time.

"I am not **kidding**, Geronimo," he whispered. "Look behind you."

I rolled my eyes. I was getting tired of these silly tricks. Still, I turned around anyway. "See, I told you . . ." I began.

But I didn't get any further. That's because for once, Trap wasn't joking. I was face-to-face with a **gigantic, enormouse, mega-huge crab!**

I had never seen anything like it. This crab was bigger than fifty sumo rat wrestlers!

Remain calm, I told myself.

I took a small step backward, then another. The crab kept its BEADY little eyes trained on me.

Only a few more pawsteps and I could

dive into the water. I'd be safe there.

Suddenly, my cousin sneezed.

In a flash, the crab stretched out its claw and lifted me into the air.

"**Heeeeeeeeeelp!**," I yelled. The blood rushed to my furry head.

Thea and Benjamin stuck their heads out from behind a big rock. "Hang on, Geronimo! We'll save you!" Thea called.

She pulled out a bottle of perfume. She sprayed it in the crab's eyes.

The crab blinked, confused. Then it swung me around in the air like a cat with a new chew toy.

It was not a good feeling. "**Good-bye, mouse world!**" I sobbed. "**Good-bye, family!**"

Just then, Trap hurled a coconut at the crab's head. Benjamin tickled it with a bird's feather.

The crab laughed and dropped me. Well, no, it didn't exactly drop me. It hurled me in the direction of the trees. I landed in the middle of a partridge nest. I was surrounded by a slew of openmouthed tiny birds.

"**Heeeeeeeeeelp!**" I screamed.

Just at that moment, the mother partridge arrived. She had a **BIG, FAT WORM** in her beak.

I opened my mouth to scream. But before I could squeak, she dropped the worm in my mouth!

I spit it out in disgust. The mother partridge looked insulted.

"I am not a baby bird. My name is Stilton, *Geronimo Stilton*," I tried to explain.

The mother partridge just squawked. Then she pushed me out of the nest. I landed with a thump on my head.

"Oh, why couldn't we go to the *Soft Squeak Resort*?" I **MOANED**. I needed a nice cheese dinner. I needed a good night's rest. I needed an ice pack for the lump on my head.

THUMP . . . FLOP!

That night, I was so tired, I fell right to sleep. At midnight, I woke up with a start. Something had woken me . . . but what?

That's when I heard a very peculiar sound. Thump . . . flop! Thump . . . flop! Thump . . . flop!

It sounded like someone walking. But these were no ordinary pawsteps. A picture from the pirate guidebook flashed before my eyes—the **GHOST OF SILVERPAW**. He had one good paw and one paw made of metal.

I gulped. Was the ghost of SILVERPAW really haunting Thump Flop Island?

Benjamin was awake, too. He grabbed my paw. "Uncle, maybe it's the GHOST!" he whispered.

I tried to look brave. "Don't worry, my dear little nephew," I said in my most confident voice. "I'll take care of it."

Now if only someone could take care of me. I felt faint with fear.

Cautiously, I trotted toward the beach.

Just as I'd thought. A long row of very strange pawprints dotted the sand. Who could have left them?

A Coconut on the Head!

Right then, I saw a **large** shadow.

"Yum, yummy yum, yummy yum yum!" it sang.

It was gnawing at a coconut.

I moved closer to get a better look. That's when it hit me. The coconut shell, that is. Yep, that ghost threw the shell right at my head. HOLEY CHEESE, that hurt!

I cried out in pain. Then I fainted. When I came to, the ghost was gone.

The next night, I heard the ghost shuffling around on the cliffs.

Thump . . . flop! Thump . . . flop! Thump . . . flop!

I knew I had to do something. So I crept

up behind him. He was gnawing on a roasted crab. I inched closer. Oops! The ghost spotted me. He took aim and launched the crab shell at me.

Clunk! He hit me right between the ears. Nice shot. Could this be the ghost of a professional mouseball player? I thought it over for two seconds. Then I fainted.

The following **night**, I hid behind a sand dune. This time, I had a plan. I was going to surprise the ghost. That's right. No more fainting for this mouse.

At the stroke of midnight, I heard his pawsteps.

Thump . . . flop! Thump . . . flop! Thump . . . flop!

This time, he was slurping on a mango.

It was so strange. I had no idea ghosts

liked to eat. I wondered if they sometimes ate the leftovers from my mega-huge fridge. I always blamed Trap when my leftovers mysteriously disappeared. But maybe it was a ghost! Now I would finally find out the truth.

I was getting **excited**. After all, I am a newspaper mouse. I like to get the scoop.

With a squeak, I jumped up from behind the sand dune. "P-p-p-paws up!" I stammered. "D-d-don't move and you won't g-g-get hurt!" I hoped the ghost couldn't tell I was petrified.

Seconds later, the *PIT* of the mango caught me right between my eyes. *I WENT DOWN LIKE A BOWLING PIN.*

When I came to, the ghost was leaning over me. His eyes glowed in the moonlight. Could it be? I blinked. Yes, it was. I was staring at the ghost of Rough Rat Ricky — otherwise known as Bouncer!

The ghost's eyes glowed in the moonlight.

A Ghost!

The ghost leaned toward me. "Yo, Mousey Mouse!" he shrieked at the top of his lungs.

I shook my head. Even as a ghost, ROUGH RAT RICKY, aka BOUNCER, was still just as loud. I was frightened out of my skull. "B-B-B-Bouncer, you're a G-G-GHOST!" I squeaked.

I opened my eyes really wide. I had never seen a real live ghost before. **Sure**, I've had lots of near misses. Like when I was trapped in an old mansion that appeared to be haunted by cats. Or when I was chased through subway tunnels by an oversized phantom. But this was the first time I'd ever been snout-to-snout with an honest-to-goodmouse GHOST!

My fur stood on end. My knees felt weak.
Then I noticed something strange. Bouncer
wasn't floating in the air. And you couldn't
see through his body. In fact, he looked
just like he always did.

"Ho, ho, ho! I'm no ghost, Mousey
Mouse!" Bouncer snickered. "You've been
reading too many spooky
stories!"

I watched as he
stuffed his face with
an entire pineapple. No,
a GHOST wouldn't eat
food that way. But a real
LIVE Bouncer would.

It turns out Bouncer had been living
on the other side of the island. He had
sprained his ankle when the plane crashed.
He'd made a *CRUTCH* to help him

walk. Can you guess what his pawsteps **SOUNDED** like?

Thump. . . flop!

Thump. . . flop!

Thump. . . flop!

OYSTERS
ON THE HALF SHELL

That night, we celebrated Bouncer's return with a delicious meal. Here's the menu:

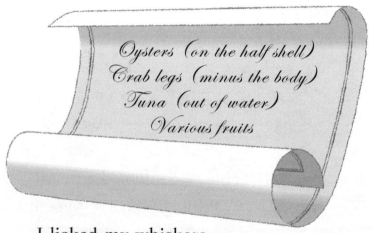

Oysters (on the half shell)
Crab legs (minus the body)
Tuna (out of water)
Various fruits

I licked my whiskers.

Cheesecake! I was so hungry, my tummy was rumbling in three different languages. I decided to start with the oysters. But when I bit into one, I heard a horrifying **CRUNCH!**

"SLIMY SWISS BALLS!!"

I shrieked. I had **CHIPPED** my tooth on something. I spit the nasty object into my paw. I could hardly believe my eyes. There in my paw lay an enormouse, glittering white pearl! Thea quickly opened the other oysters. Each one contained a pearl!

Trap's eyes were shining with excitement. **"We're rich! We're rich!"** he sang. "I knew you were good for something, Cousinkins!"

rich!

ARE YOU A TEAM PLAYER?

The next morning, Trap woke me up at dawn. "Wake up, Geronimoid!" he shouted in my ear. "I've decided we need to go *SWIMMING*. No, make that YOU need to go *swimming*." Uh-oh. I didn't like the sound of this.

"We need to find more oysters," Trap went on. "More oysters. More pearls. Got it, Germeister?"

I chewed my whiskers. "Why me?" I mumbled. "Why can't you go?"

Trap shook his head. "Well, isn't that just like you, Cousin? So self-centered. You need to learn to be a team player," he scolded. "Now, I've divided our jobs. You dive for the pearls. And I'll stay on the beach and watch."

CLOWN FISH

FIGHTING FISH

MOORISH IDOL

JELLYFISH

CORAL

SEA ANEMONE

STARFISH

OYSTER

EEL

ANGELFISH

OCTOPUS

I was too tired to argue. I grabbed a basket. Then I dove into the water. It was FREEZING. Oh, where was a nice, warm wet suit when you needed one?

I dove deeper and deeper. There were many tiny colored fish around me. I swam by coral, sea anemones, starfish, octopuses, and more.

Finally, I spotted them. Hundreds, no thousands, no gazillions of oysters! I threw them into my basket. Then I swam up to the surface.

Far away, I saw Trap waving his paws in the air. What was my crazy cousin up to now? I

wondered. He was yelling something, but I couldn't understand a word of it.

It sounded like "**Shar . . . shar . . .**"

I rolled my eyes. He was probably telling me I needed to share. Share the oysters. Share the pearls. Share the wealth. What kind of a mouse did he think I was? Of course I would share these treasures with my family!

Just then, I noticed something out of the corner of my eye. **Ding!** A bell went off inside my brain. Trap wasn't lecturing me about sharing. He was warning me about a giant **SHARK!**

I began to swim like a maniac.

WATCH OUT FOR SHARKS!

The shark was so **CLOSE**, I could smell its rotten breath. Have you ever passed by the seafood section in a supermarket? That is exactly how it smelled. Pee-yew!

The shark had its mouth wide open. I could see its razor-sharp teeth glinting in the sunlight. "Oh, please, don't eat me. **I'M NOT FISH FOOD**," I begged. "How about some nice tuna instead? Or maybe a couple of jellyfish?"

I didn't mean to pick on the other fish. But

1. The shark was after me.

2. Bouncer dove in.

what could I do? I was **DESPERATE**.

Just then, I heard a scream. "I'll take care of it, Mousey Mouse!" a voice called.

I looked up. Bouncer was doing a cannonball off a high cliff. He landed right on the shark's back. **Crash!** Instantly, the shark closed its eyes. Then it started snoring.

At last, I reached the beach. "It's about time," Trap snickered. He took the oysters. Then he gave me back the empty basket. "Off you go," he ordered. "And this time, you should really watch out for those sharks."

3. He threw himself on top of the shark.

4. Finally, I reached the beach!

THE OLD BOUNCER
TREATMENT

That evening, Bouncer and I walked to the **WATERFALL** behind our camp. We each carried an empty coconut shell to collect water.

The sand around the waterfall glistened in the moonlight. I picked up a pawful. No, this wasn't any old beach sand. These were quartz crystals!

We were about to return to camp when we heard some voices. We peeked over the dune. A broken-down canoe was nearing the beach. Two odd-looking mice were on board. The first was as thin as string cheese. He had **huge buck** teeth and was dressed in a MOTH-EATEN captain's uniform.

His sunglasses were held together by an adhesive bandage.

The other was as **round** as a ball of mozzarella. He wore a tiny sailor's hat and an **OLD-FASHIONED** one-piece black swimsuit. On two of his paws, he wore yellow flippers tied on with rubber bands.

While the chubby one rowed, he sang this tune:

Treasure hunters are we!
We sail across the sea.
We search for jewelry and silver and gold,
We lie and cheat and don't do what we're told.
So get out of our way,
Or we'll make you pay.
Oh, treasure hunters are we!

The chubby one looked so excited, he could hardly sit still. He **BOUNCED** up and down like a yo-yo. The canoe rocked and swayed.

"No one gets in our way, right, Cap E. Tan? Right?" he squeaked. "We'll SQUISH 'em. We'll SQUASH 'em. We'll turn 'em into cat food. Right? Right?"

The captain snorted. "Less talking and more rowing, Chatterbox Charlie," he muttered.

But the chubby one kept on squeaking. "We can't tell anyone that we have the treasure map. Right, Cap E. Tan? Right?" the chubby one babbled on. "And we especially can't

Cap E. Tan Chatterbox Charlie

tell anyone that the treasure is hidden under a rock shaped like a cannon. Right, Cap E. Tan? Right?"

The captain stood with his paws on his hips. "**Quieeeeeeeeeeeeet!**" he shrieked.

The chubby one blinked for two seconds. Then he continued chattering on and on about the treasure. "Where can it be? Oh, where, oh, where, oh, where?" he jabbered.

The captain looked like he was about to explode. "**Enough!**" he cried. "Why don't you dive in and look for the rock? Or better yet, look for a muzzle!"

Splash! The chubby one hit the water. A few minutes later, he surfaced.

"No rocks shaped like a cannon! Just rocks shaped like rocks!" he announced.

The captain scratched his head. "Hmmm,

then we'll anchor by the island," he decided.

I grabbed Bouncer's paw. "What are we going to do now?" I whispered. Something told me these rodents weren't looking to make friends.

Bouncer was gnawing away on a hunk of pineapple. "I can always give them the old Bouncer Treatment, Mousey Mouse," he offered.

I chewed my whiskers. "The old BOUNCER TREATMENT?" I asked.

"Sure," Bouncer snickered. "First I tie up their whiskers. Then I shave off their fur. Then . . ."

I quickly shook my head. I wasn't into violence. That's no way to solve a problem. "We just need to get them off the island," I told Bouncer.

A GLITTERING
WHITE GHOST

Bouncer CAME UP with a plan. "Wait for me here, Mousey Mouse," he said. Then he took off.

In the meantime, the two scoundrels had reached the island.

"Forward MARCH!" ordered the captain.

The chubby one lit an oil lamp. He grabbed a shovel and started trudging through the sand.

I cringed. They were headed straight for me! But where was Bouncer?

Just then, I heard a rustling sound behind me.

A white ghost emerged from the shadows. He was moaning, **"SCRAM! MOVE IT! GET LOST!"**

I opened my mouth to scream, but my vocal chords were frozen.

Then the ghost whispered in my ear. "Pretty good, huh, Mousey Mouse?"

I should have known. It was just Bouncer. Before I could respond, he galloped down the path. **"SCRAAAAAM! MOOOOVE IT!** he howled in a spooky voice. GET LOOOOST!"

When the two crooks saw him, they turned white. "A ghost!" they cried.

They tore down the path and jumped into their canoe. They paddled away so fast, you'd think they were in a speedboat.

"I rolled in the quartz crystal sand," Bouncer told me. "Pretty cool, huh, Mousey Mouse?"

It was then that I noticed the crooks had lost their treasure map.

"'*Under the rock shaped like a cannon, the treasure is found,*'" I read aloud.

I was curious. Was there really a treasure?

Bouncer scratched his head. "**Er** . . . I'll bet my fur I've seen that rock somewhere around here," he mumbled.

Do You Love Gold?

We decided to take a look. Bouncer searched everything on one side of the path. I searched the other.

I tiptoed into the dense bushes. My teeth were CHATTERING. Who knew how many poisonous snakes were watching my every move, getting ready to bite me. Or strangle me. Or invite me to the family barbecue as the main dish!

I was about to turn back when I noticed a PECULIAR rock. Moley cheese! It was shaped just like a cannon. It was covered with moss and vines.

By the light of the moon, I could just make out words carved into the stone. It was a strange riddle.

DOES MY TREASURE MAKE
YOU WANT TO SING?

DO YOU LOVE GOLD MORE
THAN ANYTHING?

IF SO, THEN LOOK
AROUND CAREFULLY.

NOTHING IS AS IT SEEMS,
YOU SEE.

TAKE A SEAT AND LOOK
AROUND.

WHAT'S THAT HIDING
UNDERGROUND?

ONCE YOU FIND IT, YOU
WILL SEE

MY TREASURE IS JUST
LIKE A HOME TO ME.

I scratched my head. What could it mean? I sat down on a stone that looked like a seesaw to think.

Suddenly, it began to *MOVE*. A big hole opened up in the ground. Now, where did that lead? I am not a brave mouse, but my curiosity got to me. I decided to take a little peek. But as soon as I set paw in the hole, the stone closed over my head. I was stuck like a rat in a trap!

"*HEEEEEELP!*" I screeched. Oh, how do I always get myself into these terrifying situations? I'm a good mouse. I'm considerate. I help older rodents. I'm kind to mouselings. Well, there was that one time I pulled little Billy Bratfur's tail. But he asked for it. He was picking on my dear nephew Benjamin.

Bouncer's pawsteps broke into my thoughts. "Where are you, Mousey Mouse?" he called.

I jumped to my paws. "UNDER HERE!" I yelled. "Look for the **TRAPDOOR!**"

"You lost your ear in a trapdoor?" Bouncer replied.

I began to chew my whiskers. "Sit on top of the stone seesaw!" I tried.

"Stone paw?" Bouncer said. "You found a paw?"

I hung my head in my paws. Rancid rat hairs! We could go on like this forever. I'd be old and gray before Bouncer found that trapdoor. Just as I began to sob, the door opened.

"There you are, Mousey Mouse!" Bouncer cried. "Your ear looks fine. Now, where's that paw?"

DID YOU SEE A GHOST?

Two strong paws reached down and pulled me out of the hole. It was my cousin Trap. Thea and Benjamin were right behind him. My screams of terror must have woken them up. Did I mention I'm afraid of the **dark**?

Meanwhile, Bouncer was jumping up and down with excitement. "What was under there, Mousey Mouse? You look a little pale. Did you see a ghost? Come on, let's go down."

He stuck a **BRANCH** into the trapdoor to hold it open.

I was still frightened, but I have to admit, I was also curious. What was down below? A treasure chest?

Bags of gold? Sparkling gemstones? A family of ghost pirates?

I shivered. At least I had my family with me. My grandma Honeywhisker always said there's safety in numbers. If we ran into TROUBLE, we could protect one another.

Together we gathered in front of the trapdoor. Bouncer led the way.

"Last one in is a rotten rodent!" Trap snickered, pushing me ahead of him.

We headed down a very long staircase. Down . . . down . . . down . . . we crept.

BOUNCER led the way. He was holding a candle. The FLICKERING light cast spooky shadows against the walls.

CHEWY CHEESE BITS! I WAS SO SCARED, I STOPPED BLINKING.

Finally, we reached the end of the

staircase. That's when I heard a rustling sound. Then warm, soft, **HAIRY** wings brushed against my fur. That could only mean one thing . . .

A Bat!

"A **BAT!**" I squeaked. I flung my paws in the air. I guess that scared the bat. He got his claws tangled up in my fur. He seemed FROZEN with fear. I could feel his whole body trembling. I was trembling, too.

"Listen, just let go and we'll both be happy," I coaxed the bat. Instead, it hung on for dear life.

I groaned. This is what I got for not taking Bat as a second language in school. No, I had taken Teddy Bear Hamster instead. And of course I never used it. How many Teddy Bear Hamsters do you know?

Benjamin's small voice cut into my thoughts. "Hang on, Uncle Geronimo. I'll help you!" he cried.

In a flash, he untangled the bat from my fur.

I was so relieved, I almost fainted.

Thea slapped me on the side of my snout. "Don't faint, Gerry Berry!" she commanded.

Trap was right behind her. "Don't faint, Germeister!" he agreed, slapping the other side of my snout.

Bouncer threw a pail of **FREEZING** water on my snout. "Don't faint, Mousey Mouse!" he bellowed.

I shook my head. "Enough!" I screamed. "I FEEL FINE!"

At that instant, a stalactite hit me on the head like a bullet. I was out cold before I even hit the ground.

A LUMP AS BIG AS A BALL OF MOZZARELLA!

When I came to, I felt the **lump** on my head. It was the size of a giant ball of mozzarella. I'm talking family-size portion.

Thea, Trap, Benjamin, and Bouncer rushed to my side.

"He looks like he's about to faint again!" Thea shouted.

I quickly jumped to my paws. "I'm fine," I squeaked. No one was going to slap this mouse around again.

We continued on our way down a dark, rocky corridor.

Suddenly, the passageway began to get light.

Finally, we reached the **BOTTOM**.

"**Holey cheese!**" we all yelled at once.

We were in an immense underground cavern filled with water. The walls were made of dazzling quartz crystals. The water below SHIMMERED in their light. **Colored** fish darted in and out. It was a magical sight.

But there was an even bigger *Surprise*. At the center of the cavern sat an **ENORMOUSE** galleon. It was a genuine pirate ship!

I could hardly believe my eyes. Then I noticed the name of the ship. It was called . . . *Treasure*.

I took out the map and stared at it. "Under the rock shaped as a cannon, the treasure is found," I read aloud. I looked up

at my family and Bouncer. "Cheesecake!" I squeaked. "The ship is the treasure!"

The ship is the treasure!

HEAVE . . . HO!

With a **SPLASH**, Trap dove into the water. Nothing gets my cousin moving like the mention of a treasure.

"Brr . . . the water's **FREEZING!**" he screeched as he paddled toward the ship. "Am I still moving? Am I still breathing? I can't even feel my own fur!"

I rolled my eyes. *Trap really should consider becoming an actor,* I thought. He's the most dramatic rodent I know.

When he reached the ship, Trap lowered a small ladder for the rest of us to climb.

"Now we can sail home!" Thea squeaked.

Meanwhile, Bouncer and Trap tried to lift the anchor. **Heave . . . ho! Heave . . . ho!** It was so heavy that it wouldn't budge.

A galleon was a warship or a cargo ship with various decks. It had three or four masts with square sails. It sailed during the fifteenth, sixteenth, and seventeenth centuries and was suitable for long voyages.

But just at that moment, something totally strange happened. The ship began moving all by **ITSELF!** The masts rose into the air. Minutes later, the galleon drifted out of the mouth of the cavern and headed out to SEA!

Was the ship haunted? Or was there some **LOGICAL** explanation? There was no time to think about it. I ran to help Trap and Thea with the sails. The ship **SHOT OFF** like a cat in an attic full of mice.

"Want me to be the pilot?" Bouncer

The galleon drifted out of the cavern . . .

. . . and headed out to sea!

asked, reaching for the steering wheel.

"NOOOO!" we all shouted at once. Thea pushed Bouncer aside and grabbed the wheel. "I'll handle this," she said.

Meanwhile, Benjamin was busy drawing a sketch on a banana LEAF. It showed a picture of the pirate ship in its secret hiding place.

"That's very good, Nephew," I told him.

Benjamin beamed. "I just had the best idea, Uncle," he said. "You can use it in your next book."

"What **book**?" I asked. It felt like years since I had sat down at my desk to write.

"The book about this adventure," Benjamin grinned.

Hmmm . . . a book about deserted islands, pirate ships, and treasure. Maybe Benjamin was right. It did sound like an *exciting story.*

STONE SEESAW

ROCK SHAPED
LIKE A CANNON

STAIRS

GALLEON WITH ITS
SAILS FOLDED

VINES THAT COVER
THE ENTRANCE TO THE
CAVERN

*Benjamin drew this picture of the
galleon's secret hiding place.*

THE ISLAND'S LAST SECRET

The ship glided off into the warm southerly winds. The breeze felt great rippling through my fur. It felt good to be out on the open sea. I guess I'd had enough of Thump Flop Island. I was looking forward to going home.

I took one last look at the island. That's when I heard the sound. No, it wasn't a seagull squawking. It wasn't a monkey chattering. It sounded like . . .

Thump . . . flop! Thump . . . flop!

I gulped. Was it the GHOST of Silverpaw? Did he really live on Thump Flop Island?

I smiled under my whiskers. I guess everyone has a right to a secret. Even an island!

SILVERPAW'S SHIP'S LOG

By now, the island was far behind us. Thea quickly began to bark out orders.

"Trap, you'll do the cooking. BOUNCER, you'll be in charge of the sails. Benjamin, you'll keep the cabins neat and tidy. And Geronimo, you'll search for the navigational controls," she commanded.

"Aye aye, captain," Trap muttered sarcastically. But he hopped to it when Thea looked at him. My sister can be a little SCARY when she wants to.

I headed for the pirate's CABIN. There were swords and sabers hanging on the walls. An oil painting glared at me. It was a picture of the pirate Silverpaw.

How STRANGE. For some reason, he looked so familiar.

I opened the desk drawer. So many papers! What a **mess**. Old Silverpaw really needed a secretary. Thank goodness for my secretary, Mousella. Without her, I would never get anything done at *The Rodent's Gazette*. She keeps me organized.

I leafed through the logbook. It showed all of the voyages the ship had taken. It also mentioned the tons and tons of gold seized.

I wondered where all of that gold was now.

Then I found a family album of sorts. When I opened it, I could hardly believe my eyes.

*There were swords and sabers
hanging on the walls.*

On one of the pages

was written

the name

Stilton!

SOMETHING FAMILIAR

I kept **READING**. And I soon discovered that the great-great-great-great-grandfather of my great-grandfather was a *cousin* of the pirate **Silverpaw**!

Jumping gerbil babies! That meant I had **PIRATE BLOOD** in my veins. I glanced at the picture of Silverpaw. For a second, I wondered what I would look like with an eye patch. Maybe I could try one on when I got home. Geronimo the Pirate. I sort of

liked the sound of it. It made me feel *ROUGH* and *RUGGED*. Not at all like my usual self.

"Have you found the controls yet? What's taking you so long, **Cheesebrain**?!" my sister screeched.

I raced upstairs. So much for rough and rugged. I couldn't wait to tell Trap, Thea, and Benjamin what I'd discovered.

My relatives seemed **proud** to have pirate blood in their veins.

We were still talking about pirates when Ben interrupted us.

"Come look!"

he called. He had finished polishing the ship's brass fixtures. They were brilliant!

In fact, they looked as if they were made of . . . GOLD!

"Cheesecake!" Trap squeaked. "It *is* GOLD!"

Yes, everything on the ship was made of GOLD. The doors handles, the faucets, the pots — even the anchor!

So that was why the ship was called TREASURE. It really was worth its weight in gold!

I proposed donating the ship to the NATIONAL MOUSEUM OF NEW MOUSE CITY in the name of the *Stilton* family. "It is an important moment in our family's **history**," I explained. "It will be great to share it with all the rodents on Mouse Island."

Our past, for **good** or for **bad**, belongs to **us**. We need to know it in order to know ourselves better.

BLACK CLOUDS ON THE HORIZON

The following morning, I found Bouncer and Trap in the kitchen. Trap was cooking and Bouncer was eating. Well, I guess you could call it **eating**. He looked more like a food processor stuck on HIGH SPEED. Bouncer was shoveling food into his mouth so fast, his paws were a blur.

"Yo, Mousey Mouse," he called to me. "Your cousin and I have decided to open a seafood restaurant when we get home." He held up a soupspoon with what looked like some oysters in it. "Want to **taste**?" he asked.

I shook my head. The last time I ate seafood cooked by my cousin, I got horribly sick. I was in the bathroom half the night.

PIRATE SOUP

INGREDIENTS FOR 4 MICE:

4 pounds cleaned clams
and oysters
3 tablespoons oil
1/2 onion, chopped
2 garlic cloves

4 tomatoes, peeled and
chopped
toasted mini bread slices
parsley

PREPARATION: *In a skillet, sauté the onion and garlic in oil until transparent. Add the tomato and parsley. Sprinkle salt and pepper to taste. After a few minutes, add the clams and oysters. Cook over high heat until all the shellfish are opened. Place some slices of toast on each soup bowl, then pour in the soup.*

A suggestion for true pirates: Add some hot peppers to the dish!

And I wasn't reading the newspaper, if you know what I mean.

I left the kitchen and found Thea in Silverpaw's cabin. She was busy studying *ancient* nautical charts to plot out our route.

Just then, Benjamin ran into the room. "Uncle Geronimo, black clouds on the horizon!"

We raced up to the deck. Thea shook her head worriedly. "Looks like *a real storm is brewing*!" she confirmed.

We lowered the sails and substituted them with smaller ones. Now if the wind blew really hard, the ship would not pick up too much speed. We closed the portholes to prevent WATER from seeping in. Then we tied ourselves to the side of the ship to keep from being blown overboard.

Did I mention I hate bad weather? It can be so wild. It can be so crazy. It can be so hard on your fur. Once I got caught in a downpour before I was about to give a speech. I was so embarrassed. What a bad fur day.

To keep our spirits up, Bouncer and Trap told us some sailor jokes. I must have been delirious because I thought they were funny.

Captain: "Throw out the anchor!"

Sailor: "But, sir, it's still new!"

A leak springs on board a ship.

The captain arrives.

Unfortunately, it is already too late.

The ship is about to sink.

The captain shouts at the cabin boy,

"Cabin boy!

When you saw that the water was coming in,

you should have called me, fool!"

The cabin boy looks surprised.

"But, Captain," he protests.

"It's not right to be rude.

I would never call you fool."

STILTON SINKS!!

By now, the sky had turned black as night. The WIND was blowing furiously.

The waves were as high as the Sky Rat Tower Bistro in New Mouse City. Rodents pay lots of money to eat there. You can see the whole city from its incredible rooftop terrace. Of course, the Sky Rat is not for me. I get a little queasy when I'm up in high places.

I was thinking about the Sky Rat as the ship bounced UP and DOWN on the water. My stomach was bouncing up and down, too. I felt as green as a piece of moldy cheese!

At that moment, a sail split in two.

"We need to take it down!" Bouncer

shouted. He quickly leaped onto the bridge.

"I'll stay here with the women and children," Trap announced.

Reluctantly, I followed Bouncer. The **ship** *tilted* dangerously to one side. Oh, what a way to go! Washed overboard into the wild ocean *waves*. I could just read the headlines: STILTON SINKS IN THE SOUTHERN SEAS! POPULAR NEWSPAPER PUBLISHER ALL WASHED UP! What a tragedy.

Still, there was no time to cry about it now. I had

a job to do helping Bouncer.

At last, we were able to lower the split sail. I had just breathed a sigh of relief when something even more terrifying happened. The rope holding my dear sweet nephew snapped in two. Benjamin was sliding into the sea!

I rushed toward him. I was able to grab his 🐾 🐾 🐾 , but he was slipping fast. Slimy Swiss balls! We were both **FALLING SNOUT-FIRST INTO THE OCEAN!**

Then a huge hairy **PAW** appeared out of nowhere. It grabbed me by the scruff of the neck. In fact, it picked us both up. Bouncer grinned. "No time for swimming, Mousey Mice," he said with a chuckle. "In case you haven't noticed, there's a terrible storm going on!"

At last, the sky began to clear.

"The worst is over!" my sister announced. "The storm is passing."

I was so happy, I kissed everyone.

Even Bouncer and my annoying cousin Trap.

WONDERFUL, FABUMOUSE MOUSE ISLAND!

Finally, one morning we spotted an **island**. Oh, I'm not talking about any old island. This was the best island on the whole planet. **Wonderful, fabumouse Mouse Island!**

We drifted past the Statue of Liberty holding up her piece of cheese. Today she seemed to be smiling right at us.

Ah, it felt so good to be home at last!

I glanced at the others. Even Trap had tears in his eyes. After one big group hug, we twisted our tails together and shouted,

"Nothing can stop the Stilton family!"

The crowd on land stared at us openmouthed. I guess we must have looked strange. After all, it's not every day a pirate ship sails into New Mouse City Harbor.

"We are donating this pirate ship of **Silverpaw's** and its precious cargo to the good rodents of New Mouse City!" I announced.

Everyone clapped.

"Hurrah for the Stilton family! Hurrah for New Mouse City!" they cheered.

A Surprise Telephone Call

Do you want to know how it all ended?

Silverpaw's ship became a splendid floating museum. It was dedicated to the history of pirates.

Old mice and young came to visit. Yes, it was quite the tourat attraction. Trap bought a pirate costume and gave private tours for a small fee. Leave it to my cousin to cash in on our good fortune.

Thea decided to take another vacation. Guess where she ended up this time? The *Soft Squeak Resort*. Of course, she had a fantastic time. There's nothing like the *Squeak* for a relaxing getaway. And knowing my sister, she probably met dozens

and dozens of admirers there.

As for me, I was thrilled to go back to work. No more **DANGEROUS** adventures for me. I'm too fond of my **TAIL**.

One day, I got a call. "Yo, Mousey Mouse!" a voice squeaked on the other end. "It's your old pal, **ROUGH RAT RICKY**, aka **BOUNCER**. Listen, I'm coming to visit you."

All of a SUDDEN, I felt a giant headache coming on.

"My mom can't wait to meet you. And my twelve little cousins are so excited, they can hardly sit still," he continued. "Better stock up on the cheese, though. These crazy rascals will eat

My little cousins are so excited.

you out of house and hole!"

I tried to squeak. But no sound came out. Stars swam before my eyes. Bouncer and his whole family were coming to stay with me? There was only one thing to do.

I fainted.

If you are ever stranded on a desert island, it is useful to know a few survival techniques. But the most important thing is to maintain nerves of steel and never to lose heart!

How to figure out where you are when you're lost:

On a cloudless night, you can get your bearings by observing the stars. The brightest star in the Northern Hemisphere is the North Star, which is part of the constellation Little Bear (or Ursa Minor). To identify it, you must first find the Great Bear (or Ursa Major), which is also known as the Big Dipper. Start with the last two stars of the Great Bear. Multiply by five the distance between these two stars, and if you continue in a straight line, you'll arrive at the North Star, which will always point you to the north. If you live in the Southern Hemisphere, you can get your bearings using the Southern Cross. Its direction will always point south.

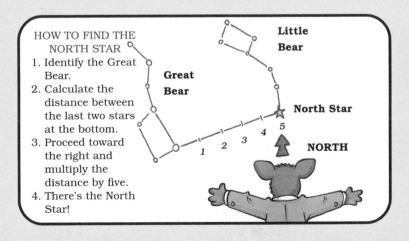

HOW TO FIND THE NORTH STAR
1. Identify the Great Bear.
2. Calculate the distance between the last two stars at the bottom.
3. Proceed toward the right and multiply the distance by five.
4. There's the North Star!

Little Bear

Great Bear

North Star

NORTH

Trail Marks: If you wish to leave some signs for those who follow you along a path, this is what should be done:

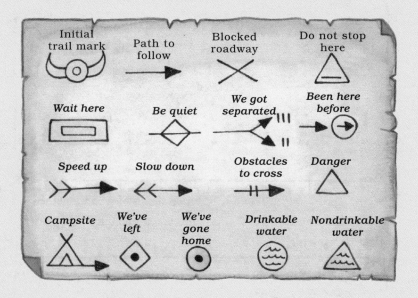

Initial trail mark

Path to follow

Blocked roadway

Do not stop here

Wait here

Be quiet

We got separated

Been here before

Speed up

Slow down

Obstacles to cross

Danger

Campsite

We've left

We've gone home

Drinkable water

Nondrinkable water

How to make a compass: If you don't have a compass, take a bowl, fill it with water, and wait until the water is still. Drop a small piece of paper at the center so that it floats without touching the sides. Place a needle on top of the paper. The paper will turn. When it stops, the needle will point north.

1. With sticks

2. With stones

3. With a lens or mirror

How to light a fire: **1.** Rub two pieces of wood together **2.** or strike two flint stones **3.** or concentrate the sun's rays with a lens or a mirror!

Gather banana or palm leaves . . .

place them on the structure of the branches

Where to find shelter: Build a structure made of branches. Then place banana or palm leaves on top. Spread twigs on the ground to keep out dampness.

How to fish: In theory, you can catch fish with your hands. . . . Try, it is not so easy!

ATTENTION: MANY TROPICAL FISH ARE POISONOUS. STAY AWAY ESPECIALLY FROM THOSE THAT HAVE BRIGHT COLORS!

ABOUT THE AUTHOR

Born in New Mouse City, Mouse Island, Geronimo Stilton is Rattus Emeritus of Mousomorphic Literature and of Neo-Ratonic Comparative Philosophy. For the past twenty years, he has been running *The Rodent's Gazette*, New Mouse City's most widely read daily newspaper.

Stilton was awarded the Ratitzer Prize for his scoop on *The Curse of the Cheese Pyramid.* He has also received the Andersen 2000 Prize for Personality of the Year. One of his best-sellers won the 2002 eBook Award for world's best ratlings' electronic book. His works have been published all over the globe.

In his spare time, Mr. Stilton collects antique cheese rinds and plays golf. But what he most enjoys is telling stories to his nephew Benjamin.

Want to read my next adventure?
It's sure to be a fur-raising experience!

MY NAME IS STILTON, GERONIMO STILTON

Have you met my assistant editor, Pinky Pick? She is only fourteen years old, but she is one of the cleverest mice I know. If you've ever wondered how Pinky came to work for me at *The Rodent's Gazette*, this is the book for you. It's a *looooong* story . . . and one that's full of adventure, laughs, and, of course, lots of embarrassing moments for yours truly, Geronimo Stilton!

Don't miss any of my other fabumouse adventures!

#1 Lost Treasure of the Emerald Eye

#2 The Curse of the Cheese Pyramid

#3 Cat and Mouse in a Haunted House

#4 I'm Too Fond of My Fur!

#5 Four Mice Deep in the Jungle

#6 Paws Off, Cheddarface!

#7 Red Pizzas for a Blue Count

#8 Attack of the Bandit Cats

#9 A Fabumouse Vacation for Geronimo

#10 All Because of a Cup of Coffee

#11 It's Halloween, You 'Fraidy Mouse!

#12 Merry Christmas, Geronimo!

#13 The Phantom of the Subway

#14 The Temple of the Ruby of Fire

#15 The Mona Mousa Code

#16 A Cheese-colored Camper

#17 Watch Your Wiskers, Stilton!

#19 My Name Is Stilton, Geronimo Stilton

and coming soon

Geronimo's

Joke Contest

Do you like telling your friends jokes that make them squeak? So do I! And I'm always looking for new jokes. Send me a few of your favorites, and I'll send you a fun gift. If you make me laugh out loud, your joke may appear in one of my future bestsellers!

Send your **JOKE** along with your name, mailing address, city, state, zip code, and birthday to me at the following address:

Thundering Cattails, I Want to Make Geronimo Stilton Laugh Out Loud!
c/o Scholastic Inc.
557 Broadway
Box 711
New York, NY 10012

THE RODENT'S GAZETTE

1. Main Entrance
2. Printing presses (where the books and newspaper are printed)
3. Accounts department
4. Editorial room (where the editors, illustrators, and designers work)
5. Geronimo Stilton's office
6. Storage space for Geronimo's books

Map of New Mouse City

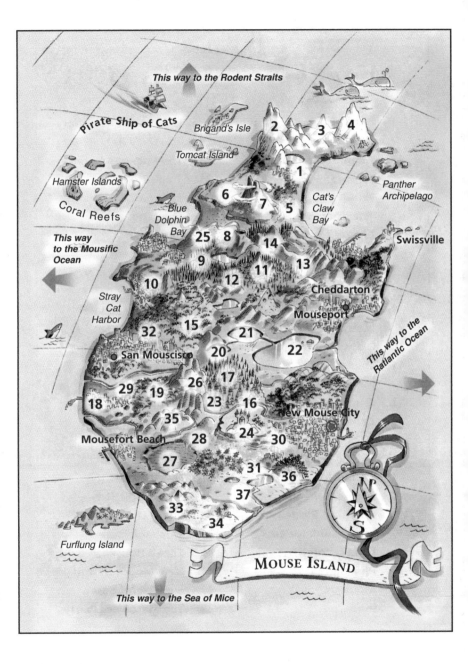

This way to the Rodent Straits

Pirate Ship of Cats

Brigand's Isle

Tomcat Island

Hamster Islands

Coral Reefs

This way
to the Mousific
Ocean

Blue
Dolphin
Bay

Panther
Archipelago

Swissville

Cat's
Claw
Bay

Stray
Cat
Harbor

Cheddarton

Mouseport

This way to the
Ratlantic Ocean

San Mouscisco

New Mouse City

Mousefort Beach

Furflung Island

This way to the Sea of Mice

MOUSE ISLAND

N
E
W
S

Dear mouse friends,
Thanks for reading, and farewell
till the next book.
It'll be another whisker-licking-good
adventure, and that's a promise!

Geronimo Stilton

Map of Mouse Island

1. Big Ice Lake
2. Frozen Fur Peak
3. Slipperyslopes Glacier
4. Coldcreeps Peak
5. Ratzikistan
6. Transratania
7. Mount Vamp
8. Roastedrat Volcano
9. Brimstone Lake
10. Poopedcat Pass
11. Stinko Peak
12. Dark Forest
13. Vain Vampires Valley
14. Goose Bumps Gorge
15. The Shadow Line Pass
16. Penny Pincher Lodge
17. Nature Reserve Park
18. Las Ratayas Marinas
19. Fossil Forest
20. Lake Lake
21. Lake Lake Lake
22. Lake Lakelakelake
23. Cheddar Crag
24. Cannycat Castle
25. Valley of the Giant Sequoia
26. Cheddar Springs
27. Sulfurous Swamp
28. Old Reliable Geyser
29. Vole Vail
30. Ravingrat Ravine
31. Gnat Marshes
32. Munster Highlands
33. Mousehara Desert
34. Oasis of the Sweaty Camel
35. Cabbagehead Hill
36. Rattytrap Jungle
37. Rio Mosquito

Dear mouse friends,
Welcome to the world of

Geronimo Stilton